I
Want
My
Mommy!

For Charlotte, with my love

~ T C x

For my lovely friend Yvonne, and her mummy

~ A E

Originally published in Great Britain in 2013 by Little Tiger Press Ltd

ISBN 978-0-545-75756-0

12 11 10 9 8 7 6 5 4   18 19/0

Printed in the U.S.A.   40

First Scholastic printing, May 2014

I Want My Mommy!

by Tracey Corderoy

Illustrated by Alison Edgson

SCHOLASTIC INC.

Arthur was playing dragons when his mommy came in.

"Look, I'm flying!" Arthur giggled.

"Oh!" smiled Mommy. "What a busy little dragon! Are you ready to go to Grandma's house?"

"**Rargghh!**" roared Arthur grumpily.
"But I want to stay with YOU!"
　　He'd never been apart from Mommy
for the whole day before.

"You can show Grandma your dragon suit!" said Mommy. "You'll be *just* like her toy dragon, Huffity."

"Huffity!" Arthur cried. "I can play dragons with Huffity! Let's go!"

When they got to Grandma's
house, Grandma gave Arthur a
big hug.

"What a cute little dragon you
are!" she said.

"Just like Huffity!" Arthur
cried, and he ran inside
to find him.

But soon it was time for Mommy to go.

Arthur held up his little nose for a special Mommy good-bye.

"Rubby noseies," whispered Mommy.

"Rubby noseies," sniffed Arthur.

Then he waved and waved until Mommy was gone.

"Would you like to paint
a picture?" Grandma asked, but
Arthur just wanted Mommy.
"**Rargghh!**" he grumped.
"Dragons don't paint!"

"Or we could make dragon music?" smiled Grandma, banging on a drum.

"OK!" said Arthur. Dragons *did* like drums.

But then . . .

ding - dong!

went the doorbell.

"**Mommy's back!**" Arthur cried.

But it *wasn't* his mommy.
"**Rargghh!**" grumped Arthur.
"Dragons don't want LETTERS!"

"It's all right," said Grandma softly. "Mommy will be back later."

Arthur gave a little dragon sniff.

"Look, Arthur!" said Grandma. "I've got some treasure. But I need a brave dragon to protect it."

"Me!" cried Arthur. "I'm brave!" He would hide it in a cave.

He ran into the backyard to find one.

When Arthur had found the
perfect dragon cave, he sat in it
with the treasure.

"Hee hee!" he giggled. No one
would find it here!

Then suddenly, he
heard another . . .

ding-dong!

"**Mommy!**" cried Arthur,
running inside.

But it was just Grandma's friend, returning an umbrella. "**Rargghh!**" grumped Arthur. "Dragons don't want UMBRELLAS!"

"I think it's lunchtime," Grandma said.
They sat together at the table.

"Mommy will be back very soon,"
smiled Grandma. "But until she gets here,
I know a game we can play!"

Grandma put a towel around her shoulders.
"Look, I'm a knight!" she cried.
"This is my cape!"
"And this is my sword!"
"Wow!" Arthur gasped.
"Hey, I want to find some treasure!" Grandma-Knight smiled.

"**Rargghh!**" giggled Arthur-Dragon. "You won't get mine!"

He raced to his cave to protect
his shiny treasure.
  "Grandma-Knight's coming to
catch you!" Grandma chuckled.

"Hee heeeeee!" squealed
Arthur, as she tickled his tummy.
Then they played knights and
dragons all afternoon, until . . .

ding-dong!

"I hope they're not looking for treasure!" laughed Arthur and Grandma, running to the door.

"**Rargghh!** I'm a brave dragon and you can't come in!" giggled Arthur.

But, when the door opened . . .

"Mommy!"

cried Arthur.
And Mommy gave
Arthur a great big hug!

"Did you have fun?" she asked him.
"Lots and lots!" said Arthur.
"Dragons love playing with their
grandmas so much. But *no one*
gives hugs like Mommy!"